THE WEAVER OF STARS

OLIVIA PEARSON

COVER ART BY LULU

PRINTED BY LULU IN THE UNITED STATES OF AMERICA

FIRST PRINTING, 2018

PUBLISHED BY OLIVIA PEARSON

ISBN 978-0-578-42829-1

Chapter 1

Red and orange leaves danced above my head in the crisp autumn breeze, tousling my strawberry blonde hair as I walked along the sidewalk leading away from school. I could hear my classmates talking and laughing in groups together, their voices mingling with the sounds of wind rustling through trees and the occasional car passing by. But as usual, I was only partially conscious of any of those things; far more of my attention, as it so very often was, was focused on the book I was reading.

I guess in that way among others- a star-shaped birthmark on my wrist, complete lack of any social skill whatsoever, a fondness for sewing- I've always been just a bit on the strange side. Stories to me are like portals to other worlds, escapes from my problems, ways of learning and enjoying things I could never hope to experience myself done by characters I could only dream of meeting. And of course, they're so much easier to deal with than people- *they* don't constantly tease and exclude you just because of the things you're into.

Easier to deal with than *most* people, anyway. There are just two real people in the world who have intrigued me, have managed to mean more to me, and I have wanted to be like more than any fictional hero. It was one of them, the one that I had lost, it so happened, who had first started me on books, really- my mother. She was the kindest, wisest, and most loving woman I've known. Strongest and most hardworking too- not just anyone could leave an abusive drunk, taking their infant daughter with them from Manhattan, New York, to live in Galena, Illinois. But she had somehow done it.

I think that it was her, more than anyone else, that accepted my odd little peculiarities. Everyone else- including myself- had either been confused or frustrated by them. But not Mom. For some reason, she had actually liked them. They had made her smile, made her laugh; I still didn't understand it.

Loss mingled with grief stabbed into my memory of her like a knife. Why couldn't she be here with me? Why had it been so rainy that night? Why couldn't the brakes have worked a little bit better?

Then, the tears came. Not very many, but they came. The mark on my wrist flashed by as I tried to wipe them away. I missed her so much. It didn't matter that I was fifteen, or that it had been four years since the accident- the pain was still there, just as sharp as it had always been.

The bell above the oaken door jingled cheerfully as I pushed it open to enter my grandfather's antique shop. He beamed at me from behind the dark mahogany desk at the back of the store as his pale blue eyes, the same color he had given to my mother and she to me, twinkled affectionately.

I grinned back. Something about Grandfather and his shop has always seemed . . . magical to me. Maybe it's the numerous artifacts that seem to have been taken directly from select moments in the past, each so different from the last and special in its own unique way. It could also be the comforting, old-fashioned ambiance, the result of so many pieces of history being crammed into one small place- or maybe it's the ancient, wise, and gentle little man who runs it, always smiling and kind. Most likely, it's a combination of all of the above.

"There you are, Lucy!" Grandfather exclaimed in his familiar Russian accent, tottering over to me and laying a shriveled hand on my shoulder. "Take a look at this!" he said, steering me towards a golden birdcage resting atop a stand. "She arrived just a few hours ago from-" His voice abruptly stopped. He cast a keen, searching glance over my face, turning it slowly with his leathery fingers so he could see better. "Have you been crying?"

I sighed. Grandfather may be old and nearly blind in one eye, but he's still pretty observant. "I was just thinking . . . about Mom."

He nodded solemnly. "Your mama was a good woman... and you are a good girl." He conveyed so much more to me than what he actually said. I knew he understood how much I missed my mother- she had been his daughter, after all.

"Eh . . . come now. She would want you to be happy, malen'kiy," he said to me, offering me a small smile. "Are you going to help me now?"

I gave him a watery smile of my own and nodded. "Okay."

"Good! Now, help an old man move some new pieces from the back out here."

I followed after him, letting our work drown out my sadness the way I knew it would till five o'clock, when we would retreat back to our apartment for the night. My grandfather continued speaking to me in his quiet, calming way, slipping between English and Russian in the way I found so amusing. Soon, I found myself snickering- he always knew how to make me laugh, even when I was a tiny child. And after I lost my mother, that ended up being a thing of critical importance.

Chapter 2

I walked among the towering wooden shelves and deeply inhaled the musty, dry scent of paper, old and familiar - the library is like a sanctuary to me, a safe haven far away from all of life's problems. I can still vividly remember when my mother would take me here.

The process certainly evolved. When I was very little, too young to know how to read, she would take me by the hand and lead me to one of the large, red pieces of velvet furniture in the corner (we called it the "Velvet Corner") and read me stories from children's books for an hour. If I still wanted to hear more- and I almost always did- we would check out books, sometimes as many as twenty, to take home with us.

To teach me how to read, she selected small, easy picture books for me to read aloud to her. Usually, these lessons took place in the Velvet Corner, or our apartment, but sometimes to make it more interesting, my mother would take me to the park or a restaurant. After this, I was the one who did the choosing, sometimes asking for her recommendations, reading increasingly long and difficult stories and simultaneously loving and gaining new knowledge from each one. Looking back, I truly feel that those were the happiest times of my life.

But after she died, things changed. I no longer had my mother to care for me and teach me, and so my grandfather moved into our apartment in her place to take care of me. There were frequent- and frightening- phone calls from my father. I went from naturally quiet and shy to downright reclusive and depressed for around two years. But the old library, with the Velvet Corner, was always there through it all.

Finally, I came to the book I wanted. I took it gently by its dark green spine, the golden letters glittering as I pulled it from its place in the shelf- and found myself looking at a large, lanky hand, suspended in its place!

I peered through the opening the book had left to look at the person on the other side of the shelf and found myself staring into a pair of dark brown eyes set in a handsome face. The boy looked to be around my age, perhaps a little older, but his expression was serious as he stared at me with a disapproving, almost arrogant look.

"I'm sorry!" I exclaimed. I could feel my face reddening but tried to ignore it. "I didn't-"

"No. It's okay," he said, holding up a hand to silence me. We stood there, rooted to the floor for a while before he sighed, like he thought I was really hopeless. "You're still holding the book."

My cheeks became somehow redder as I contemplated what I should do. We had both reached for the same book, but I had happened to grasp it first. It was my right to keep it, wasn't it?

Yet it would be so much easier to just let him have it. I sighed softly and handed it to him.

"Here. Sorry again," I said quietly.

"Don't worry about it," he answered before striding off.

I sighed again, louder this time. Why had it been so easy for that guy to walk all over me? Why did I have to be so timid?

Around thirty minutes later, I had selected several other books and was just coming to the librarian's desk, when I stopped in my tracks. Just in front of me was the boy from earlier!

I could see him better now- he was not very tall, standing only around an inch or so taller than I did, and remarkably slim. His messy, straight black hair partially covered his right eyebrow, and he wore a hoodie with jeans. I looked at his stack of books, quite a formidable assembly... and the dark green one amongst them.

"Will you be needing anything else today, Mr. Atlas?" the librarian asked as she handed him the last book.

"No, thank you," he said. His somewhat deep voice was polite and clear, but also icy and emotionless.

He walked away, back ramrod straight. I moved up in the line to check out my books... and walked right into him! He had stopped short to adjust his armload of literature, and now I found myself helping him pick novels up off the floor.

"Uh... I'm really sorry," I mumbled, trying to avoid his gaze.

"It's fine." His voice was calm, but his eyes professed his irritation. He was probably thinking something along the lines of, 'This klutz again? Who even is she?'

He stood up finally, giving me a final parting glare as he moved away. I stared after him, feeling just a bit regretful; leave it to me to earn the hatred of a total stranger.

Chapter 3

Even though it was a Saturday, Grandfather and I were still kept relatively busy running the antique shop. Shining, cleaning, selling, and unpacking are all divided between the two of us. Not that I mind- I find the work to be relaxing. It gives me something to focus on.

I was just finishing up applying a coat of furniture polish to a seventeenth-century table, when Grandfather emerged from the back room, carrying a small box.

"Take a look at this," he said to me as he placed it in my hands.

I ran my fingers lightly over the smooth wood, silently admiring the skill of the carpenter. I lifted the lid to inspect its contents and there, all neatly packed inside, were materials for sewing.

There was a long, silver needle, sharp and shining, pearly white buttons, clear and sparkling in the sunlight, and a little pair of golden scissors. The gorgeous black and blue thread seemed to come in every thickness and texture imaginable.

"It's an embroidery box," Grandfather explained. "It came yesterday while you were at school, but I wanted to clean it before showing it to you."

"And all of this was inside?"

"Yes. It came just like that."

I took out one of the spools of thread and held it up close to my eye. "Where did it come from?"

"A boy came by yesterday and dropped it off. He said I could have it for free."

"That's strange. It seems very old . . . and it's in great shape."

He shrugged his shoulders. "I suppose. I was thinking you might like to have it."

"Really, Grandfather?" I asked him, in awe of the fact that he would just give something so precious away so easily, even to me.

"Why not? I paid nothing for it. And I'm sure you'd have far more use for it than I ever would."

"Thank you, Grandfather!" I exclaimed, hugging him. He laughed and ruffled my hair.

"Ah, don't waste your time here!" he ordered, "Go back to the apartment! Make some use of your gift, eh?"

I nodded and hugged him one more time. "Thanks,

Grandfather. I really do love it."

A smile broke out across the wrinkled face. "I know."

Chapter 4

I sat cross-legged on the floor of my little room, leaning against the bed. The materials the box had come with were slightly peculiar- all in either very deep blues or blacks. The buttons were lovely in both color and quality, far too much so to be used on just everyday clothing. And yet, there wasn't very much thread; the spools were quite little . . .

Perhaps I would make a sort of small quilt . . . yes, that was it. The thread's dark shades . . . they were perfect for a night sky . . . that would work splendidly.

And so, with something of an idea in my head and strange but wonderful tools at my fingers, I started my work.

Late that night, I had gotten up to use the restroom. In the still silence of the night, I passed by the window, glancing outside to look out into the dark, star-speckled scene beyond, and my heart almost stopped; I was looking at an exact replica of the quilt I had sewn earlier.

I stayed up all night, looking up at the sky and comparing it to my work. There was not a single difference- in the place of my white buttons, stars shone brightly above. The dark blue color I had used was the same one the sky boasted. Everything was identical.

I examined the embroidery box and its contents- other than seeming to be very old and in excellent condition, there was nothing so different about them compared any other set of sewing materials I had ever seen.

I ended up spending two hours on my cell phone. I researched the situation in as many ways and on as many websites as I could, but still came up completely empty-handed. Should I tell Grandfather? No. What could he do? He was as clueless as to the embroidery box as I was, probably even more so. He wouldn't be able to help. No, I was left to unravel this mystery on my own.

Chapter 5

If there was one place I could look to for answers, it was the library. I had selected various volumes about stars that fateful morning, and was just starting in on the first in the Velvet Corner, when someone said the following.

"So, Cornelius was right. You *are* the third Starweaver."

I looked up in surprise . . . and found myself staring at none other than Mr. Atlas!

I stammered for a moment, trying and failing miserably to find the correct words. But "Mr. Atlas" held up his hand. He seemed to do that a lot.

"Save it," he said coolly. "I take it you're curious to learn more about the embroidery box?"

I nodded, unsure of what else to do.

"Well, then I suggest you come with me," he said. And with those words, he sauntered away without once looking back. I stared dumbly after him for just a moment before jogging to catch up, leaving a mountain of astronomy books resting on the scarlet sofa.

My new guide was leading me rather quickly through the small town. I felt the need to at least try to initiate some conversation.

"What did you say I was? A Starweaver?"

He nodded. "Yes. Don't worry. Cornelius will explain it to you."

"What's your name anyway?"

"Jonah. Jonah Frederick Atlas. You don't have to tell me your name, by the way. I already know- Lucy Anastasia Penstark, right?"

"How did you know that?" I asked, startled.

"You'll see when we get there," he answered.

Eventually, we left town and found ourselves trekking through the woods. Everything inside me was screaming not to go any further- what was that thing about going anywhere with strangers? What would Grandfather say? What if something happened?

But still, my curiosity outweighed my better judgment. I continued to follow Jonah. After several minutes of walking in random, zigzagging patterns, Jonah stopped. Looking furtively around us, I saw him take out what looked to be a necklace of some sort- at any rate, it was a silver chain with a deep blue stone attached to it.

"Hold on to me," he commanded. The order, however, was so unexpected, I was slow to comply. He sighed, frustrated, before pulling me towards him. My entire face felt on fire as he held me against himself. Then, he put the necklace around his neck. Leaves started to fly around us in a swirl, trees swayed with sudden wind, the

forest itself spun like a top . . . and that is when I shut my eyes from

fright.

Chapter 6

I opened my eyes to find that we were standing in the midst of remarkably soft, springy grass, dotted with brightly colored flowers. I could smell salt in the air and hear the crashing of waves against rock- we were somewhere close by the sea.

I realized I was still clinging to Jonah. Quickly, I disengaged myself and tried to brush off the awkwardness.

Jonah did not seem to care too much, though. He just dusted his clothes and turned away.

"Come on. We're going in there," he said, pointing with his finger. And that's when I saw it.

Jonah had pointed at a large building nestled in a little thicket of trees, flowers and vines scaling the brick walls as it rested proudly atop a cliff. About half of the roof, I could see, swelled up into a dome-like structure, and the glass that covered it had been peeled back, as though someone was looking up at the stars. It looked ancient and mystical, old as time itself and just as mysterious.

As we walked off in the direction of this impressive structure, I looked up and was completely amazed by what I saw. I could see stars- billions and billions of stars in more patterns than I could ever hope to count, all glittering and sparkling in that stunning patchwork of night skies. That's what it was- a collage of night skies, all joined together here in this place.

"What is this place?" I asked Jonah, beyond intrigued.

"It's called Star Rock," he said, not bothering to so much as turn around. "The sky here is called the Mosaic, and the house is Night Hall."

We finally came up to Night Hall's wooden front door. Jonah peered through the miniature stained-glass window above it and knocked, but he had hardly lowered his fist before the large door swung open to reveal a tall teenage boy, beaming at us from inside.

"Jonah! You're finally back!" he exclaimed. He was bursting at the seams with energy and optimism, golden curls bouncing with every movement and bright green eyes snapping as he spoke.

"Oh!" he exclaimed as his gaze fell on me, "You brought her!"

Jonah nodded. "Lucy Anastasia Penstark, meet Ryan Garrote Blackstone."

Ryan offered me a friendly smile and stuck out his arm for a handshake. "Nice to meet you," he said. I could only return it with a polite greeting.

"Come in, come in!" he said as he ushered us inside. I only had a fraction of a second to glance over my shoulder at the Mosaic, the flowers, and the trees before the door swung shut behind us with a decisive click.

Chapter 7

I found myself trailing after the boys, listening to them talk. Or rather, listening to Ryan talk and joke while Jonah gave quiet, simple answers to his many questions. It was quite an interesting thing to observe; the two teenagers were so very different, like night and day, summer and winter, and yet they apparently shared a deep bond of mutual camaraderie and trust.

The large circular room they led me to, located on the left side of the house, was apparently an observatory of some sort, and no doubt the dome I had seen earlier. The first thing one noticed about it was the numerous strange items that had been stuffed inside; some hung from the ceiling, while others lay strewn about the room. There were so many you could scarcely even walk without running into or stepping on one. Just a single place remained completely uncluttered- a flight of stairs that led up to a landing, upon which stood an ornate and very expensive looking telescope, its huge, unblinking eye fixed upon the sky. And looking through that telescope was a tall, bent figure.

"Cornelius?" Jonah called up to him. The man turned and I saw his face fully in the moonlight. He was an elderly man with hair that had long since turned gray and clothed in a long, brown tunic. Over his shoulders and arms, and reaching all the way down to his feet, was an olive colored robe, decorated with orange, black, and dark green designs all over. A very old man, old and yet alert- there was a certain pensive, thoughtful quality in the careworn face, an astute intelligence that veiled a kind, noble heart.

As soon as he saw me, a look of astonishment came over the aged face and he hastily descended from his height.

"Cornelius, Jonah brought her back!" Ryan said excitedly. "This is the third Starweaver!"

The man, Cornelius, looked closely at me... then, finally, he spoke.

"Lucy- for that is your name, isn't it?"

I nodded.

"Lucy, do you have any peculiar birthmarks anywhere on your body?"

I was quite shocked by the question.

"It's okay. You'll see," Ryan whispered, flashing me a reassuring smile.

"Uh... yes, sir," I answered. "Here... on my wrist."

Cornelius eagerly took my hand and held it close to his face.
Ryan had to stifle a laugh at the shock on my face. Even Jonah allowed
a slight upturning of his lips.

"And out there... I want you to pick out the pattern you
designed last night." He motioned to the telescope as he spoke. I took
it as a signal to ascend the landing and look for my own sky. After
several minutes, I found it. When I informed, he only muttered, "So,
we were right. You *are* the third. If you weren't, you would never be
able to find it, much less make it the way you did..."

"Excuse me, sir?"

He looked at me with a weary expression on his face, like I
was inconveniencing him.

"Could you possibly explain to me what's happening? I
mean... could you-?"

I couldn't get the right words out. But, somehow, Cornelius
understood. He sighed, rubbing his face with a hand, and eventually
nodded.

"I know what you mean. I'll do my best to explain everything
to you."

Chapter 8

"A Starweaver is someone responsible for making the tapestries that form the night sky. Every single night, they come here to weave them on looms. As soon as they are finished, they will take them off the looms, sew them together, and the pattern they have created together is copied into the sky."

"There can only be a total of three Starweavers at one time. They come here every day until they turn fifty years old, at which point they are no longer able to do so. All of them do this except for the best and most skilled of the three. That person, instead of being released from their duty, earns a new one; they must teach and guide the next three Starweavers until each has reached twenty-five."

"Every Starweaver is born with a star-shaped mark somewhere on their body. That is how we tell which children are possible candidates."

"It's true," Ryan interjected. "Mine is on my thigh, and Jonah's is on his neck."

Cornelius nodded, apparently used to being interrupted. "Yes. You see, not everyone can be a Starweaver. Whether or not your work will be translated into the night sky depends on two things- the thread, and the person. The thread is supplied to us by the mainland once a month, but as to who weaves it... they must be born with the ability to correctly use it. The birthmark is the first sign of this odd gift."

"The Teacher- that is the title given to us- constantly watches out for any children born with it. Then, somehow, in some way when they find one, they manage to get the embroidery box to them and have them use its contents. If the pattern they choose- which, if they truly are a Starweaver, would be a night sky- appears in the Mosaic, for it records all, then the Teacher brings them here and has them identify their work. If they pass this final test as well, they become apprentices."

"When I first took in Jonah, he was ten... and I found Ryan less than a year later. But, still, we needed one more Starweaver. And that, my dear Lucy, is where you enter the equation."

I took a step backward, trying to understand was happening. "What if," I eventually brought myself to say, "What if I choose not to?"

"Then, there shall be only two Starweavers until they both reach the age of fifty and the cycle repeats itself, with the better

Starweaver becoming the Teacher in my place and the other simply returning to his life," Cornelius answered.

Everyone in the room seemed to hold their breath waiting for my response. It was an unusual feeling for me- strangers never cared this much about what I had to say.

I thought about my options. I could say yes, and hope for the best, adjusting into a new responsibility I had apparently been born to fulfill. But I could just as easily say no, forgetting any of this had ever happened and leaving Cornelius, Jonah, and Ryan to sort out the problem on their own.

There wasn't really much to consider in my eyes.

"I'll do it. I'll do my job as a Starweaver alongside Jonah and Ryan. It would be my honor."

Chapter 9

My response affected everyone differently. Cornelius let out a relieved sigh. Jonah calmly folded a lock of hair behind his ear, but his almond-shaped eyes showed there was much on his mind. Ryan whooped and spontaneously threw his arms around me.

"Well," Cornelius eventually said, "You should leave now. Your grandfather might worry. Just come back tomorrow. And tell no one of your new life."

He took a necklace from his pocket and gave it to me. It was a large green stone which I saw, mounted upon a rose gold chain.

"Put that on whenever you need to come or leave here," he instructed. I nodded, remembering the necklace I had seen Jonah put on.

"Nice color," Ryan commented. "Mine's red on gold, and Jonah's is blue on silver."

"Uh... thanks," I answered, still not used to Ryan's unusually friendly and inclusive nature. It was rare for me to interact with someone this open and straightforward.

"Bye, everyone," I said timidly. Ryan, of course, waved and beamed. Cornelius shook my hand. Jonah just stared at me.

After going outside into the field, I took a deep breath and pulled out the necklace. I paused only a moment to admire it before putting it on.

As my slim fingers turned over the brilliant green jewel on its rose gold chain, I absently stared down at the thoughtful face reflected in the emerald, running the events of the day before through my mind like a film reel. It almost didn't seem real to me, like the vague memory of a favorite childhood book, or the dim recollection of a story your grandmother used to tell you before bed. Had I not been fingering the necklace at that moment, I could have believed it to be a dream, it was so fantastically unrealistic and foggy in my mind. Jonah, Ryan, Cornelius, Star Rock, Night Hall- I could have easily imagined it all. And yet, here I was, holding the precious stone in my hand, struggling to get my head around it all.

Lost in thought, I sighed and leaned back against my cream-colored bedroom wall, which was sprinkled generously with little pink roses. I still remembered painting them on next to my mother, her hand tenderly guiding my brush strokes as we added tiny petals to each flower.

I had felt my heart break the night I lost her forever, felt it break and suffered through the pain of its shards slicing into me from the inside. I had done my best to live with the deep void they had cut out of my soul, leaving a huge piece of it missing, for the past couple of years. But now, I felt that void was finally being filled. For the first time in years, I didn't feel so dreadfully alone.

I found myself once again standing in the grassy field and listening to the sound of the ocean. But this time, instead of looking up at the Mosaic, I was looking up at a clear, bright blue sky. I could feel the sun's warmth bathing my limbs, a nice contrast to the cool of the tangy breeze.

The serenity was divine as I made my way towards Night Hall. I could see even from a distance how much less frightening it looked in the daytime. The beige stones and rusty red roof, the green vegetation, and the pink and purple blossoms had all been highlighted by sunlight. Now, instead of menacing, the building appeared tranquil, a mansion in a small cluster of trees, watching over the flower field from its perch on the sea cliff. It was a nice start to my new life.

Chapter 10

"Hey, Lucy! Welcome back!" Ryan exclaimed in his friendly, upbeat way as he welcomed me inside Night Hall.

"It's good to see you, Ryan. You too, Jonah," I said, offering a shy smile to each of them.

"Cornelius says we're to give you a tour of the building," was all the black-haired boy said without returning my smile. He wasn't rude exactly, but he certainly didn't seem happy to see me. "Come. We don't want to take too much time from the weaving itself."

He walked off, giving a slight motion for Ryan and I to follow him.

"Don't mind him," Ryan comforted me. "Jonah's not the most... friendly guy in the world. But, he's really smart, and when it comes down to it, he's pretty nice too. You just have to get to know him a little is all."

I nodded to show him that I understood. In the next few minutes, the boys managed to show me the entire house, which included a library- Ryan laughed at how enthusiastic I became about it- which was furnished with lavish purple furniture, huge bookcases, and an ancient looking piano, a room for storing sewing materials, and a room with three looms in its center, tapestries hanging all over the place. It was here my work was to be done.

"Come on, Lucy!" Ryan said, taking me by the hand and leading me to the loom at the center. Jonah followed to oversee the lesson.

"What happens if I mess it up?" I asked nervously.

"Don't worry, you won't."

I was surprised; the remark had come from Jonah.

"How do you know?"

"Because you're a Starweaver. You were born with a gift for this," he stated. "And a gift only needs hard work to become success. We have the first ingredient accounted for. The remaining question is are you willing to work hard?"

I looked at him with newfound respect. Ryan agreed with him. "So, are you?"

My gaze shifted between the boys before I responded by sitting up straighter and saying, "Yes. I am."

What Jonah had said was indeed true. I had a natural talent for weaving, and I did my best to absorb all the boys taught me. Before very long, I was able to produce a relatively decent cloth of my own. When I had finished sewing on little designs and buttons, Ryan clapped and cheered like he was at a football game.

"Yeah, Lucy! We knew you could do it!"

Jonah, for the first time since I had known him, truly smiled. It was a very nice smile, made all the more pure by its rarity. It gave me the sense I had indeed accomplished something worth celebration.

"Now, let's move on to the *real* thread," Ryan said, taking my work from the loom and handing me a box of materials. I nodded resolutely, trying to soothe my nerves.

"You already made one night sky with the embroidery box," Jonah said in my ear. "This one just has to be bigger is all."

I nodded again before getting to work. My friends watched me in silence, paying close attention to everything I did. To my surprise, the apprehension vanished as I worked. It was satisfying to watch my fingers delicately weave the thread, to produce something beautiful like this all on my own- I was having fun.

"Try putting more of your own feeling into it," Ryan suggested.

Jonah nodded. "Right. You are creating art now, Lucy. You are expressing yourself to all the people who will see this sky. That's what art is- expressing your emotions, your opinions, your style, in some way, shape, or form to your audience."

The sky itself was soon completed. Now, I would have to add in stars. As I selected some buttons, Cornelius walked in.

"She's doing really well," Ryan informed him. "She's working on her first real sky right now."

"Just adding the stars," I said as Cornelius neared my loom. He looked at my tapestry, gently running his hand over its soft surface.

"Not bad at all," he said approvingly. "Boys, you may start working now." Jonah and Ryan obediently went to their own looms on either side of me to begin weaving. "But," the Teacher said, turning to look at me sternly, "You must be extra... passionate, especially at this stage of creation."

"What do you mean?" I asked, a little confused.

". . . Do you know what stars are to people, Lucy?" he asked after a moment.

"No. What?"

"They are beacons of hope. Lights in darkness. Flickers of happiness in the midst of pain."

Chapter 11

Eventually, each of us had finished our shares of work respectively. Now, we all sat together on the floor, sewing them together to form the one final tapestry that would serve as sky tonight.

"So, Lucy," Ryan started, "Jonah says you're from a really small town."

"Yeah. Galena, Illinois. It's small, but really nice, especially during this time of year. What about you? Where are you from?"

"Well, I actually live in Switzerland. But apparently, my father was British, hence the name."

"Apparently?"

Believe it or not, Ryan actually became somber. "I . . . I never really knew him . . . it's just been my mom, my stepfather, half-brother for a long time now."

"I'm sorry," I said. I felt awful. I hadn't meant to bring down the mood by any means.

Luckily for me, Ryan understood. "It's fine. And anyway, it's not your fault at all."

"Your English is really good, by the way," I offered apologetically. I was surprised to learn Ryan wasn't American. His accent and vocabulary were spot on.

"I could say the same about your German," he said, laughing. His peals of laughter only grew louder at the bewildered look on my face.

"All Starweavers understand each other, no matter what language they're speaking. It sounds to me like you, Ryan, and Cornelius are speaking in German. And to Jonah, it sounds like we're speaking Korean."

"You're Korean?" I asked, turning to him. Jonah nodded.

"Yeah. I live in Seoul, actually."

"But your name doesn't sound very-"

"That's because it's not my real name. Jonah Frederick Atlas was a character from a book I read when I was little. I liked the name way better than my real one, so I decided to go by it."

I would have asked him for his real name, but the look he shot me made me decide against it. Besides, I could definitely relate to idolizing a fictional character like that.

"Done!" Ryan proudly announced as he held up the tapestry for us all to see.

It was the skillfully made product of hard work blended with natural talent. Each thread had been thoughtfully woven to match the others, making a sort of harmony formed by our fingers rather than our voices. The three of us worked well together, and I could just imagine how the sky would look that night- a sleek, velvety black darkness, broken occasionally by burning starlight. And people gazing up to the heavens, in awe of the serene work of art hanging right over their heads, drawing wonder and peace from something we had created. The thought filled me with elation.

That glorious vision of what would and could be, that glassy-eyed dream we shared, passed through all our minds that sunny afternoon. It was a somewhat emotional moment for us, looking at the first of the many beautiful tapestries, the sparks of inspiration, the beacons of hope we would make together, not only as a team or as colleagues, but as friends.

Chapter 12

The magnetic beauty of the waltz, both elegant and yet intense in its complexity, drew me from Night Hall's front door all the way to the library. I knew the powerful, foreboding music could only be coming from the timeworn piano inside- but who could possibly be playing it? Careful to make as little noise as possible, I pushed open the door and was spellbound by what I saw.

There, seated in front of the piano in the corner, was Jonah, his fingers flying over the black and white keys with graceful strength in a showcase of both remarkable skill and breathtaking passion. He seemed to be giving me a glance into his very soul, each individual note receiving his full attention and being used as a little conductor of what was going on inside his head.

It was then that I came to understand a bit more about Jonah Atlas. He wasn't the distant, chilly person I had first taken him for. On the contrary, the icy, unruffled demeanor was only a thin curtain draped over the raging, complex emotions that lurked just beneath, a facade that hid deep, profound sentiments that only ever revealed themselves when their owner was weaving tapestries or creating music. Jonah wasn't a statue; he was the sculptor. A refined, talented artist who best articulated his feelings through his art.

The piece ended. The pianist lowered his hands, a nostalgic sigh escaping from his lips. Then, he turned around, a hint of startlement flashing in the almond-shaped eyes that came to rest on me.

"I'm sorry," I quickly blurted out before he could say anything. "It's just that the music was so good... you were amazing."

Jonah, oddly enough, seemed to disagree. "I'm nowhere near as good as my sister was." His eyes misted over, cloudy with the sudden memory of her. "She was so . . . wildly expressive. I learned from watching her play when I was a toddler, but I still can't imitate her style."

"Whoa, seriously? Jonah, you're a genius! That kind of gift isn't something common!"

The only response my praise received was a frown.

"I still can't hold a candle to her. I don't think I'll ever be able to play like she could."

It was my turn to shake my head now. "Jonah, you weren't playing- you were painting. I could almost see the colors of the notes as you pressed the keys. And regardless of how good your sister was, your job isn't to be like her. It's to be yourself, and to tell your own story through your own music. And you did just now. You told your story clearly and so well to me without even realizing it. If that isn't talent, I don't know what is. And-"

Jonah held up his hand to stop me. "Thanks." His tone was calm and even, but his lips curled into a brilliant smile of heartfelt gratitude and ecstatic joy. "Really- thanks."

After we had finished our tapestry that day and Jonah had left, I told Ryan of my encounter with him. He listened intently before saying, "Yes. Jonah is an incredible pianist. Definitely the best I've ever heard. He really wants to be a virtuoso someday."

"Why not now?" I asked. "He could easily make it."

"He has two younger sisters, a younger brother, and one more sister who's older than he is, but there's something wrong with her... I think she's autistic or something."

"The older sister? The really good pianist?"

Ryan nodded. "Yeah. That's what he means when he calls her so expressive. Music is the only language she's fluent in. It's the only way she *can* really communicate anything."

"Anyway," he continued, "Jonah wants to help their parents take care of his siblings for as long as possible. As a matter of fact, he was reluctant to become a Starweaver just because he was worried he wouldn't be able to see them as often."

I understood. "What about you?" I asked Ryan. "Do you have a dream?"

He nodded, a mischievous glint coming to the emeralds in his face. "Come with me."

Chapter 13

Ryan led me down to the beach, with Night Hall looking down at us from its great height. We walked along the sandy shore, the ocean to our right and the cliff face to our left until finally, we came to a huge cave in the rock, a wide river of seawater flowing into its open mouth.

"Come on," he said to me excitedly, "My dream's in here."

I hesitated only a second before following after him.

I've always been slightly afraid of caves. Something about them has made me nervous for as long as I can remember. Fortunately, we did not have to go very far into this one before we came upon what Ryan wanted me to see.

There, painted with bright colors and carved with immaculate attention to detail, was a wooden ship, bobbing peacefully in the underground lake. I was stunned.

"Ryan... *this* is your dream?"

He stood beaming. "Yep. Granted, she's pretty small, but still, not a bad one."

"Did you build this?"

"Of course not! When I first came here, I found it while I was exploring Star Rock. It was just a drab, broken down heap of a ship. But I managed to fix it up. Jonah helped too. We even repainted it. And one day, when the time is just right, I want to fly her!"

"Did you say fly her??" Now I was really interested.

"Yeah! Here, the ships don't only sail- they fly through the air! I'd love to just go soaring through the sky, over the mainland, over the sea, over mountains and rivers and valleys..."

A dreamy, distant look came over Ryan's face. It was obvious he craved adventure; more than likely his decision to become a Starweaver had been a very easily made one.

"Well, I'm sure you will one day," I said.

He sighed wistfully. "I sure do hope so."

Chapter 14

The fruity tartness of berries pleasantly mixed with the sticky sweetness of syrup in my mouth as I took a large forkful from the stack of pancakes before me. I washed it down with a long sip of coffee, enjoying the deep, rich taste thoroughly warming me from the inside out. Gingerly, I set the steaming mug next to the topaz hairpin that lay glittering on the dining table- a birthday present from Grandfather, who had, as he did every year, allowed me a day away from the shop.

November twelfth. I was sixteen.

The Mosaic, with its sparkling white stars scattered across the charcoal expanse of sky, hung high above our heads, silently gazing down on us with unmoving eyes as we stood together in the flowers.

"So, what is it?" Ryan asked in his usual, careless manner. "Is something wrong, or-?"

"Happy birthday." Jonah's brown eyes shone in the darkness.

"How did you know?" I asked.

"The clip in your hair. And anyway, you never text unless it's important," he answered simply. "It couldn't have been anything bad- your face is too happy."

"Oh, wow! Happy birthday!" Ryan said joyfully.

I grinned at the both of them. Ryan had more to say.

"You know what we should *really* do to celebrate?" His eyes had taken on that troublesome gleam again.

Jonah arched an eyebrow, instantly recognizing it. "What are you plotting, Ryan?"

Chapter 15

"I stole this from Cornelius years ago," Ryan said, eagerly opening a small, finely carved cabinet. "Been waiting for the perfect day to use it all this time." We were aboard the boys' ship, the Ladybird, inside what had once been the captain's cabin. The kneeling boy's golden curls seemed to jump about his head as he rifled through the little cupboard, face practically glowing with delight.

Most of the color had long ago faded from the murals along the walls depicting jubilant fairies and Elysian mermaids, and the delicately crafted furniture, with its admiral blue upholstery and intricate patterns, had been humbled by the many years. But even so, I could read the many stories of adventure and valor, of betrayal and loss etched into every lurking shadow, in each rustle of the silk drapery, just barely masked by the thin layer of dust now coating the formerly rich, splendid chamber. The tales that room could tell if it could talk! Fantastic accounts of narrow escapes, honorable crewmen, bloodthirsty pirates - and now a new one just barely unfolding, depicting three teenagers just trying to have fun and celebrate a birthday.

"You stole a wind string?" Jonah asked disapprovingly as his eyes fell on the object in Ryan's hand- a short, silvery rope with several knots firmly tied in.

"I had to! How else could I get the ship to fly?" our friend exclaimed defensively.

I didn't exactly know what a wind string was, but I guessed it was one of the many strange trinkets strewn about the observatory. Cornelius liked to call himself "a collector of the unusual and rare." Jonah simply called him a hoarder. But either way, he did have quite an impressive array of items lying around the place- he probably hadn't even noticed his wind string was gone.

After coming back above deck, Ryan bounded up behind the large steering wheel, a look of unmistakable eagerness written all over him. His alert green eyes shone as bright as the stars he wove, and his body twitched in anticipation as he impatiently bounced on the balls of his feet. I couldn't help but smile.

"Go on! What are you waiting for?" Jonah urged.

"Okay! Just hold on!" Ryan shouted back excitedly. A huge grin on his face, he dramatically untied a knot with a flourish.

A gust of wind suddenly began blowing all throughout the cave, howling against the rock walls and rippling across the water. As the Ladybird's sails began to catch air, I felt the ship lurch beneath my feet. We were moving!

"I'm untying another!" Ryan yelled, a slightly crazed look flashing across his features, quick and radiant as a lightning bolt.

Sure enough, another gust, just as powerful as the last, whistled through the cave, feeding the sails more and more wind. Above the breathtaking rush of air, my ears caught a gleeful laugh from Ryan and the warning "Hang on! He's unknotting another one!" from Jonah. One final gale was all the Ladybird needed. She was coasting down the water now, gaining more and more speed as her free-spirited young captain cackled madly from the helm.

Faster and faster down the tunnel the ship sailed, riding on the river of water flowing out to sea. Wind tore at my hair, whipping it this way and that and adrenaline coursed powerfully through my blood as we raced along, eventually coming out of the cave. For about two seconds we skimmed along the open ocean like a stone before the ship gradually began to leave it, slowly but surely rising up and off the water until before long, we were gliding above it, climbing higher and higher in the air the whole time; we were flying!

My heart was pounding violently inside of my chest, pure exhilaration filling me to the brim as I fell to the deck, the force of the takeoff throwing me off. I could see Jonah nearby, clinging for dear life to the ship's railing and just barely keeping his footing. Ryan, now steering, shouted triumphantly.

"How's this for a birthday present, Lucy?"

I was too awestruck to reply. We were really soaring through the Mosaic, far above the rippling blue ocean. I felt like I was invincible.

"We're coming up on the mainland now," Jonah called to me, still staring over the side at the landscape below- a sleepy, medieval-looking village embedded within an overgrown forest. It was like something I had only ever seen in picture books or peaceful dreams. That's what it felt like as I soared through the stars with my two best friends; a dream- the best dream ever.

Chapter 16

The ending of the day brought mellow shades of orange and pink, a nice background against the blazing sun. Its final rays dyed the ocean a metallic bronze and gave Night Hall a certain charming, warm glow, but I wasn't admiring the scenery. Instead, I was occupied with struggling to talk some sense into the depressed, injured athlete sitting before me on the ancient mansion's doorstep.

"Ryan, that's absolutely ridiculous! Your ankle will be fine- it's not that bad, really. And remember, it's all just a game!" I exclaimed, my face flushing with anger and confusion. My friend just hung his head dejectedly for a response. He looked disconcertingly different from the rhapsodic boy who had so confidently steered me across the stars only a week ago; his broad shoulders sagged and his usually bright green eyes were dull and listless. And this huge change was all over being kept off the soccer team by a twisted ankle!

"Not to me, it isn't. You don't understand," Ryan now said, shaking his head and avoiding my steely gaze.

"Then make me understand," I urged, softly placing a hand on his shoulder and making my tone calm in an effort to soothe him. "Talk to me. I'll listen."

He took a moment to examine me, as though checking to see how genuine the affirmation was. Then, sighing wearily and scooting aside to allow me to sit beside him, he began to explain.

"For most people, soccer *is* just a game. But not for me. For me, it's . . . so much more."

I could feel the puzzled look my face was twisting itself into. Ryan elaborated.

"My stepfather's never really . . . cared about me. He's never been mean exactly; he just never paid any attention to me when he could help it. I guess I've always been something like . . . a background character in our house. For him, it's always been about my half-brother. Everything in our world revolves around *his* son, not some Englishman's. Almost anything I do- school, chores, games, drawing - Jean can always do it better."

"Except for soccer. At first, it was just fun. I was good at it, and I loved running up and down the field, kicking the ball over the grass, shouting at my teammates till my voice was raspy. But eventually, I started to notice that whenever I played well, he'd actually speak to me. He'd say... nice things about me, not just about Jean. He'd care what I thought or felt or said as long as I kept playing soccer well. And when I didn't, it all went back to normal. The compliments, the encouragement- the *love*- it all stopped."

"I always tried my hardest, not only because I liked to play, but because I wanted to make my stepfather proud. Maybe one day I could get him to look at me like he looked at Jean, not just after a good game, but all the time, if I just got good enough at soccer."

"I spent my childhood wondering that. I still wondered it when I was about to go to team tryouts at my high school."

"But now I don't. Not anymore. The ankle changed that." He looked down distastefully at his swollen foot. "Everything's the same. Jean's the favorite again, like he's always been and always will be."

"Soccer isn't just a game for me; it gives me a voice in my house. It gives me an identity apart from 'Jean's half-brother'. It makes me mean something."

I was completely taken aback. "Wow. I never would have guessed that about you. You're so full of light, and kind, and friendly towards everyone you meet."

He shrugged and gave a little laugh. But it didn't come like they usually did- hearty and boisterous and full of life. No, this one was quiet and carried a note of dark, almost cynical, bitterness.

"I suppose it's because I know what it's like not to be treated like that. I know how it makes a person *feel*- and I'd never wish that on someone else."

"How?" I questioned. "How does it make you feel?"

". . . Worthless. Useless. Faceless. Nameless. Unimportant. That's what I am without soccer."

I rapidly shook my head, standing up again suddenly to look Ryan directly in the face.

"That's not who you are. Someone striving for attention from someone who, judging by what you've told me, doesn't even deserve you as a son. A machine built for soccer, trying desperately to please someone cold and cruel- that's not you."

"Then who am I?" he asked, raising his head slightly.

"Someone who makes people smile. Someone who makes them feel safe and happy and loved," I answered. "You've been looking for value in the wrong place, Ry. It's about time you finally start searching where you should have- not in the pride you'll never completely get from your stepfather, but in the joy you can evoke in everyone else."

Ryan finally smiled that familiar, too-big-for-his-face grin I knew and appreciated so much.

"Yeah." Gingerly, careful not to put too much weight on his ankle, he stood up to stand next to me. "Maybe you're right."

And the two of us stood together before the huge, vine covered building in the grove of trees, staring up at the seagulls as they cut across the sunset.

Chapter 17

I found myself gradually settling into my new life as a Starweaver. The work was easy and enjoyable for me, and it felt good to experience pride over an accomplishment of mine again. As an added bonus, I grew closer to the boys each time I saw them. They quickly became my best friends.

Before I knew it, Christmas Eve had arrived. My grandfather and I had only just finished our ham and pineapple, when my phone lit up, the screen flashing Ryan's profile picture. I read the text he had sent me; 'Come to Nigh Hall.'

I wasted no time.

"Grandfather, I have to go," I called to him as I threw on a jacket and headed out into the air, stiff with wintery cold.

"At this hour? It's Christmas Eve, malen'kiy," he said, frowning slightly.

"I know," I answered apologetically. "I just forgot to do something at the library. I'll be back soon, I promise."

He nodded reluctantly. "All right. Hurry back, though."

I dashed out the door just after giving him a final wave and rushing out into the chilly December air, letting it envelope me. As I jogged down the sidewalk, buildings brightly lit with multicolored strings of lights and shimmering white snow flew by. All of it carried the festive, merry atmosphere of Christmas, from the beaming charcoal mouths of stick-armed snowmen to the wisps smoke curling up from chimneys. But it was one house, which happened to have its blinds open, which caught my eye in particular.

Inside, happily chattering and laughing together was a family not so very unlike the ones I had always pictured in dreams, or had enviously listened to classmates describe over the years. There was a father, strong and kind, a little girl perched on his knee and squealing with delight, and next to them bearing cups of hot chocolate, a mother, pretty and gay. They all seemed to be enjoying simply being with each other so much . . .

I felt a claw of jealousy jab sharply into my heart. Why couldn't *I* have been that girl? Why couldn't it have been *my* parents celebrating the holidays with me?

But I had to shove my gloom aside for now. Leaving the street behind, I ran off into the forest, to escape, at least for a while, from my darker thoughts.

"There you are! I was beginning to worry!" Ryan exclaimed as he embraced me and took me inside Night Hall.

We entered the library, now heavily peppered with emblems of Christmas. The fireplace roared warmly, the sweet perfume of gingerbread and tea wafted about the room, wreaths of holly and gleaming bells hung everywhere- and an elegant, hauntingly beautiful melody rose up from the piano as Jonah's graceful fingers carefully struck each note with angelic precision.

Bittersweet. That was the word for his music. As bittersweet as dark chocolate. As bittersweet as life itself.

Noticing us, Cornelius rose from the plum colored sofa he had been reclining on, setting down his teacup on the glass table.

"Merry Christmas, Lucy," he said, placing a ruddy hand on my shoulder.

"Come on; join us for a little Christmas Eve snack," Jonah said to me as he stood up and led me by the hand to a sumptuous armchair and set down a plate and teacup at my left and right hands.

It was one of the happiest times of my life. An informal little Christmas party spent with my best friends... and even that had an undertone of sadness. Even that was somehow bittersweet.

Chapter 18

"Let's go outside, Lucy! Bet you've never had Christmas in the Summer!"

Ryan was right about that. By now, I was used to the way things worked here- both the time of day and the weather seemed to operate completely at random. Not that I minded much.

The three of us had all shed our coats and jackets earlier and were glad of it now. We spent the next half hour splashing around in the ocean, running through the grass and sprinting and down the sand. Ryan wanted to take the Ladybird out again, but Jonah and I talked him out of it; Cornelius, we knew, was very much awake, though inside, and we did not want to risk him learning of the stolen wind string.

The three of us were now lying in the flowers, gazing up at the sky as the sunlight dried out our clothes and talking casually, when Jonah suddenly asked me:

"What's wrong, Lucy? You've been acting strange since you got here."

I had no right to be surprised. The boys, Jonah especially being naturally more observant, had learned how to decode my moods like computers by now.

"I saw... a family, on my way here. There was a Dad, a Mom, and a little girl, all so happy together . . . and I got jealous."

"Jealous of the family?" Ryan asked, rolling onto his side to look me in the eyes.

"Yeah." That was all I said for a while, before finally telling them everything. I told them about *my* father, about *my* mother, how before I met them and Cornelius, my grandfather had been the only person left who even remotely cared about me. It just felt so good to vent, to be able to tell my real feelings to people I loved and trusted.

By the end of the story, I was in tears. I'm doing way better than I was four years ago, but I still have my emotional moments. And this was one of them. I was basically ranting in between my sobs about how my only family left were an old man and an angry alcoholic I could not even remember.

I felt two strong arms wrap around me, pulling me into a hug. Ryan was gently whispering to me, "You're okay now. It's all over. You can always count on Jonah and me. We're always gonna be here for you... we're always gonna be your friends."

"Exactly," Jonah said resolutely. "You're born into a family-

you and your friends *choose* each other."

Chapter 19

Dr. Kendall shut the door behind her as she entered the room, her lustrous braided black hair pulled into a long ponytail and hanging down her back. She adjusted her glasses as she sat down, looking at the clipboard in her dark brown hands with a strange expression I had never seen her make before.

That was saying something. I had been seeing Dr. Kendall since I was four years old, and her face had always been calm, composed, and kind. Now it was deeply troubled and concerned.

"Well?" Grandfather asked, as though reading the doctor's behavior and realizing what it meant, but still needing confirmation that his guess was accurate.

Dr. Kendall sighed, a look of utmost pity and sorrow now sweeping over her countenance.

"Lucy," she said addressing me in her deep, soft voice, "The results of your tests have just come in . . ."

I nodded. For the past month, starting a few days into the new year, I had been experiencing weight loss and a dull, aching pain around my stomach. Concerned, my grandfather had insisted we go to the hospital and I get it checked out. I remember Dr. Kendall saying it probably wasn't all that serious. But judging by her behavior, it was.

"And . . .?" I prompted, almost worried she would try lying to me.

She took a deep breath and looked me straight in the face. I could see my concerned, apprehensive face, reflected in the chocolate colored eyes.

"Lucy, there's no easy way of telling you this. The results say you have cancer of the pancreas. I'm sorry."

The entire world froze. I felt numb in that moment, like I had gotten the wind knocked out of me. I was only vaguely aware of my grandfather, his face a macabre picture of horror and grief.

"Beyond that's there's not much else I can tell you right now," Dr. Kendall continued sadly. "We'll have to run some more tests; see what stage it's in-"

"What's the survival rate?" My voice was harsh and hollow, so much so even I was surprised.

Dr. Kendall winced and said in a tone that was both gentle and sympathetic, "Ninety one percent don't make it past five years, honey... I am so, so sorry."

Chapter 20

The following two months were occupied by trips to the hospital. Not that they did anything but tell me more about how terribly sick I really was. When I wasn't busy undergoing some kind of test or treatment, I was locked in my room, doing nothing, really, except allowing a cloud of depression to swallow me up the way I had when my mother died. I longed for her now more than ever. *She* would have known exactly what to do to encourage me and lift my head, know just what to say to inspire me to keep on fighting. But would I have listened? Would even my mother, as wonderful and wise as was, had been enough to drag me back to reality from the pit I'd buried myself in?

Grandfather tried not to show his extreme grief, but he couldn't help it. He felt like a failure- he had been entrusted with the admittedly difficult task of taking care of me and raising me all on his own and now, he was very rapidly losing me, powerless to do anything about it.

I let the entire world pass by without really being a part of it. I was someone observing quietly from the stands, not a player on the field. The only times I left bed were when Grandfather forced me to eat or walk around for the sake of exercise, and I only ever left the house to go to the hospital. I even stopped going to Night Hall to weave and spend time with the boys. I of course considered it many times, but always ended up deciding against it; what good would telling them I had less than a year to live do?

My phone constantly buzzed with messages from Ryan.

'Hey.'

'Where are you?'

'Are you coming?'

'Talk to us.'

'Are you okay?'

'What's going on?'

'Cornelius is worried.'

'I'm worried.'

'Even Jonah's worried.'

'You can tell us.'

'You need to come.'

'We miss you and hope you're okay.'

'Remember what we said on Christmas Eve.'

Something stirred up in me as I read that last one, partially because it was from Jonah- he had never texted me directly before. But also, because it was true; that impossibly cheery

December day, grass and flowers cushioning us as we lay looking up at the bright blue sky, the boys had given their word that they would always be there for me to lean on no matter what. And I was taking it for granted. No matter how embarrassing or disheartening it was, they *deserved* to know.

Chapter 21

Once again, I stood before the wooden door of Night Hall. It gave me a queer feeling to willingly be here in this place again when I had been pushing it, and those I knew to be inside, away for so long. What would they say? How would they react? How could I explain all the chaos of the past month?

I couldn't do it. There was just no way. I turned to go... and heard the door being thrown open behind me. A second later, I was nearly thrown off my feet by a force more like a tackle than the embrace I knew it to be.

"Lucy! There you are! What happened? We were so worried about you!" Ryan gushed as he spun me around to face him. He had changed little in the last two months- same energetic, fun loving soccer player I had known and loved so dearly...

"It's nice to see you too, Ryan," I responded. Ordinarily, I would have said it with at least a hint of a smile, but I didn't have the strength or the will to, even for one of my two closest friends. "But I'd rather tell everyone at once. Let's go inside, huh?"

Ryan momentarily caught on to my demeanor. "Okay."

I met Jonah in the library. His face, which had been quite gloomy and somber when I first entered, flickered with curiosity and joy for a split second upon seeing me, but quickly became serious and questioning again; he had read instantly that there was something wrong.

"I'm going to get Cornelius," Ryan told us before making his exit and leaving Jonah and me alone.

"I'm glad to see you again," Jonah said politely after a moment's silence.

"And I'm glad to see you too," I answered, eyes wandering listlessly from one bookshelf to another. As much as I hate to admit it, I felt . . . out of place there, like I didn't belong . . . and the saddest part was that I was the one responsible for it. I was the one who had disappeared, made them worry about me.

Finally, Cornelius arrived. He treated me like nothing had happened, like there was no rift between us at all. He seemed to be glad, but not surprised, with my presence. And so, I sat down, took a deep breath, and fessed up.

Chapter 22

"Listen, I know I no longer have any right to be here. I dishonored my agreement as a Starweaver and all of our relationships as friends, and I'm so, so sorry."

"But . . . two months ago, I was diagnosed with pancreatic cancer. It' . . . it's pretty bad. I'll be lucky if I make it to next year."

"I got low. Every single day I would just feel sorry for myself, and I felt like I couldn't let anyone, especially people I cared about, see me like this. I didn't want anyone else to worry. I saw what it did to Grandfather, and I didn't wish that on anyone else."

"So, I pushed everyone away. I wouldn't talk to anyone if I could have any say in it. I figured if I didn't talk to people, if I alienated myself as much as possible, it wouldn't hurt them as much when I was . . . . gone."

"I know I shouldn't have . . . but I did. And that's why I basically ghosted all three of you. Between treatments and depression, it's been pretty rough."

"And I don't care if you guys hate me, but I just wanted to come here to say that I am so, so sorry! You didn't deserve that, and I really, truly regret it now. I'm sorry!"

I felt like a toddler, sitting there on the purple velvet couch next to my friends and Teacher, making a total fool out of myself, but I didn't care. It felt so good to finally be able to tell them how I felt, but at the same time absolutely terrifying that they should see me like this, completely exposed and unprotected, like a hermit crab without its shell.

I felt a hand on my shoulder, providing me sudden comfort. Believe it or not, the arm attached to it belonged to Jonah.

"You don't have very long left," he said seriously, "The way I see it, you need to make the most of what little time you have remaining."

Ryan nodded and hugged me. "That's right. And we're gonna be with you every step of the way. If these *are* your last months, let's make them the best they possibly can be."

Cornelius looked me in the face. "Lucy, I want you to know that even if we are not blood family, we will always be here for you. You'll always have a safe place to come to, and people who care about you to talk with. Do you understand that, child?"

I nodded, smiling weakly for the first time since the diagnosis. "Okay . . . Okay."

Chapter 23

Despite finding new emotional strength in my friends, physically, my sate only worsened. Just a few weeks before summer started, I essentially moved in to the hospital.

They're by no means places of fun and laughter, hospitals. Everyone there has something wrong with them. And every situation is unique in its own way. But there's still a faint sense of companionship- we're all in the same boat. All of us are trapped inside bodies that aren't functioning the way they're supposed to and all of us are desperate to get them back to normal.

Take Jenny Vilkins, the twelve year old who served as my roommate the first few weeks of my hospitalization. She had cancer, like me, but instead of it being in her pancreas, it was in her lungs. She told me all about how she had once had long, beautiful blonde hair, how it used to stream out behind her as she and her older brother raced around the family farm- but now, all of that lovely hair was gone, lost to chemotherapy. She gave me the impression of being a naturally free spirited, imaginative, and good humored, but her condition- and a more personal matter- had severely watered all of that down, leaving a sad, softened girl in the place of the old one.

"My brother and I were really close," she was telling me, "But then, we found out about the cancer . . . he got so upset. He ran off a couple of months ago with some gang or something... no one knows where he is now."

I nodded. "Well, at least you have your parents. My father was an abusive alcoholic. My mom took me and we left when I was a baby. But then, when I was eleven, there was a car accident... she died. I live with my grandfather now. He's the only blood family I've got left."

"Then how are you . . . okay?" She asked, her tone sounding confused, like she was struggling to figure me out. "I can't imagine losing both my parents and then taking on... well, what we are taking on. How do you get through each day?"

"Friends," I answered plainly. "It might sound simple, but it's true. Friends might not be related to you exactly, but they're your own little chosen family. I couldn't imagine getting through this without them; believe me, I'd be a complete wreck."

Jenny pondered this carefully.

"Well," she said eventually, "I'd trade all of my friends for yours. There's *a lot* of them, but they're not nearly as nice as yours sound. I'd never call them my chosen family like you did." She sighed, a regretful, lonely little sound, "My only real friend was Ian- that's my brother- and now, he's gone."

"Hey," I said, managing a little bit of a smile and looking steadily at Jenny, "That's not true. From this moment on, you have me too."

That night as I lay in my hospital bed, I noticed a sound other than Jenny's soft snoring and the beeping of machines- it was a small, quick tapping at our window. I nearly had a heart attack (the beeping coming from the machine I was hooked up to sped up drastically) when I saw who it was; Ryan, waving and grinning.

As silently as was possible, I opened the window, allowing the both the cool summer night's air and my friend inside the room.

"What are you doing here?" I hissed.

"I just came by to give you this," he said, passing an item into my hands; an embroidery box.

"You can still be a Starweaver, even if your work will be a little small," he explained. "You're gonna have to sew whenever you can- just say it's your hobby or something. Every night, Jonah and I will take turns getting your piece of the tapestry from you. I'll come back tomorrow night to get the one you make in the morning."

"What about tonight?" I asked, worried.

"Cornelius has agreed to help us just this once, like he did before we found you. Don't worry. Just focus on getting well."

And with those words, he hugged me one last time and disappeared out the window, just as suddenly as he had appeared.

Chapter 24

As my fingers busily sewed, my ears listened intently to Jenny's chipper voice endlessly prattle on. She liked talking, but I didn't mind; I liked listening. She seemed to derive the most pleasure from sharing little details about her life, small, seemingly trivial things, like how the faded yellow walls of our room reminded her of the ones in her grandmother's farmhouse, and the way the cat in the abstract multicolored painting above her bed made her long for her own pet, a Calico kitten who liked to pass his time sunning on the windowsill.

But always, somehow, the conversation led back to Ian, the way all roads in the Mediterranean world seemed to find their way back to Rome. The pale blue curtains looked just like the ones hanging in his old room, and that wooden chair in the corner brought back memories of his childhood dream of becoming a carpenter and studying woodworking in Europe one day.

She clearly missed her brother desperately, and felt like he had abandoned her in her time of need. And she was right- Ian being there for Jenny the way Ryan and Jonah were for me could have made this terrible period in her life much more bearable.

It wasn't fair. Why should someone so good and strong like Jenny have to suffer through this without the person she loved most in the world? She was at the very least entitled to that. I wished I could somehow, someway, give it back to her.

And that's when a crazy, hair brained idea struck me; the crazy, hair brained idea that maybe, just maybe, that there was a possibility I could.

I finally laid down my needle, finished with my somewhat small tapestry. I held it up and admired my work; a deep, blue black background upon which I had sewn stars. But unlike what I had done in the past, the stars were not arranged in a pattern, but in a simple message.

'Come home, Ian. Jenny needs you.'

When Ryan came to pick up my work, his green eyes showed his surprise as he whispered frantically through his teeth, "Lucy, what's this?? Why'd you sew a message into the tapestry?? And who the heck are Jenny and Ian??"

"She's Jenny," I answered, pointing at the sleeping form on the hospital bed adjacent to me. "She has lung cancer, and Ian's her big brother. They were really close, but he was so upset when they found out about her, he ran away. And unlike me, she doesn't have any close friends."

"You're out of your mind," Ryan said, shaking his head like he really thought I was.

"Ryan!" I whispered fiercely back, frustration finally bubbling over, "I don't have much time left! I have a gift, a very rare one, and I'm not gonna waste my last year using it for everyday things or only for myself! I'm gonna use it for others- for actually *helping* them."

Ryan looked at me, confusion lingering on his face for just a moment before nodding. "Okay . . . okay."

Chapter 25

"Ms. Vilkins," a nurse said, poking her head into our room, "You have a visitor."

Jenny instantly went silent, stopping herself right in the middle of the funny story she had been telling me. She obviously had no idea what was going on.

I felt my heart skip a beat. Had it truly worked? Was this what I had been waiting all week to see? Had I done it?

Momentarily, a tall young man, his burly arms covered in tattoos and his blonde hair cut in one of the strangest styles I had ever seen, walked in, his gait slow and hesitating. It was odd seeing someone like that walk in so cautiously and awkwardly, like he was scared of being there.

But Jenny wasn't scared of him. Her fawn colored eyes, mirrors of the young man's, lit up with happiness and shone brighter still with tears. "Ian!"

The man, Ian, said nothing, just walked to the bedside of his little sister and sat down. He ran his big, rough looking palm over her smooth head like a fortune teller over a crystal ball. He blinked with disbelief several times, as if wondering if the girl lying sick in the bed was even real.

Jenny, on the other hand, needed no such assurance. She eagerly threw her arms around him, hugging him tightly like she would never let go. He waited only a moment before gently wrapping his own muscular arms around her. Then, as strange as it was, he started crying.

"I'm sorry, Jenny . . ." he breathed in a shaky voice, the words sounding like they were made of glass and would shatter in the air, "I'm so, so sorry."

And that's when I knew I had finally found what I was living my last year for.

I was finally released from the hospital. I bade Jenny, whose recovery was now going along quite smoothly, goodbye, and returned to the little apartment I called home at last.

I also was able to go directly to Night Hall using my necklace again. I don't think I've ever been more glad to be there than when Cornelius welcomed me back in, when Ryan hugged me so warmly and tightly, when Jonah had actually smiled his special, radiant grin. My work, and the happiness I now knew it could give people, soon became my greatest comfort.

Home life was no longer very fulfilling. Grandfather wasn't the same. He was quieter, sadder- and incredibly reluctant to ever let me out of his sight. Not that I blamed him; the doctors had given me no more than seven months.

When I walked into homeroom that first day of school, the first thing I noticed was the way everyone stared at me. Most of them, if not all, knew about my condition by now, and they were probably wondering what the best way to react to me was.

I smiled, just to reassure them I wasn't going to drop dead on my feet, before taking my seat. The second I did so, I was bombarded by questions.

"How are you?"

"Are you okay?"

"Are you going to die?"

"What's it like having cancer?"

"Will you be going back to the hospital?"

Students asked the kind of questions paparazzi directed at celebrities- invasive, impulsive, and far too personal. Heads turned as I walked down the corridors, revealing varying degrees of curiosity. Whispered gossip flew around classrooms at light speed. I was silent through everything, tasting the bitter irony of it all. All of my classmates, some of whom I had known since elementary school, cared about me more now that I was sick than they ever had while I was healthy. For once in my life, I knew what it was like to be the most popular girl in school.

At lunch, I was surprised to see that a seat had been saved for me. I plunked down my tray in between an artistic girl called Lacy Gardener, and the quarterback on our football team, Joe Henderson.

"So, Lucy," Joe asked, "How're you feeling?"

"Okay." I kept my gaze on my lukewarm hamburger.

"No, but really, how are you *feeling*?" He persisted. "Does it hurt?"

"Yeah," I answered, spooning up liquidy applesauce from my tray. "I have abdominal pain now. And I keep losing weight." I popped a baby carrot into my mouth.

"I wish *I* could say that!" Joked a girl with hair that was naturally blonde but now streaked with every color under the sun. "You should really give me your cancer if you don't want it!"

"Candace!" Lacy scolded, disgusted.

"What? Just trying to lighten the mood," she said defensively.

"How about we all just treat Lucy like a normal human being?" Lacy suggested, her tone showing her irritation. That was strange for her- Lacy was generally a laid back, soothing girl who passed her free time painting, not one for confrontation.

"How about you let her make that suggestion if she wants to?" The rainbow haired girl shot back.

Before I knew it, a debate had started, both girls raising their voices gradually while the rest of us at the table looked on. Eventually, I'd had enough.

"It's not contagious."

Everyone turned from the argument to look at me.

"Cancer isn't contagious. I couldn't give it to you even if I wanted to. And believe me, I don't want to and neither do you."

Somehow, everyone sensed the argument had ended.

Chapter 26

The last school bell had just rung the next afternoon, announcing the end of the day. Some teenagers fled the huge, castle-like building like it was on fire, while others lingered a while, waiting for their friends on the steps. I was about to leave myself, when I remembered a book I had to bring home . . . and was in my locker.

I had barely reached the hallway where the lockers were, in fact, when a strange sound stopped me in my tracks. To my ears, it sounded like someone was crying. No, wrong word. Like someone was *sobbing*, a sorrowful, heartbroken sound that said more than any speech ever could.

Turning the corner to investigate, I was shocked to see Lacy, sitting on the floor with her back against the wall, makeup smeared and shoulders sagging.

"Lacy?" I asked timidly. She looked up at me with a blank face, deciding how she should react to being discovered.

"Uh . . . are you okay?" I wished I were one of my friends. Ryan would know exactly how to lift up Lacy's head, while Jonah would have had some sensible advice to offer. I had neither . . . but I could listen.

She wiped her eyes and pushed her long brown hair behind her ear. "I'm fine."

"Is there anything I can do to help? It's okay; you can tell me. It's the least I could do after yesterday."

She hesitated only a moment before pouring out her heart to me.

"My parents hate each other. For as long as I can remember, they've fought. Well, it finally all collapsed. I guess they've always stayed together for my sake. But now, I'm sixteen. They think I'm old enough to handle not seeing my dad every day, with my mom seeing some other guy, but I'm not. I don't think I ever will be."

She continued speaking, rambling, more like, about them, of the vicious fights she had been seeing for years and of how she had often had to act as an intercessor between them, a very rickety bridge across a great divide. She had always struck me as a fragile girl, and this apparently was very close to shattering her delicate being. I just listened to all of it- and that was enough. I could tell she was liking getting all of her thoughts and opinions off of her chest, even if it was to a cancer-stricken introvert with months left to live.

Maybe that's why she felt so comfortable spilling so much to me; because I *wasn't* a popular, flamboyant, loud person. Maybe it was not *in spite* of who I was, but *because* of it.

I sat cross legged on the floor, sewing buttons onto my tapestry, and talking to the boys. The fact I had cancer was not one to be discussed unless I brought it up, something we had agreed upon without telling each other, and the conversation was about more light-hearted things, as it often was.

"And then after this month I- Lucy, what are you doing?" Jonah cut himself off mid-sentence, his tone going from relaxed to intrigued in a split second. He had seen that I was sewing words.

"You remember that one time I put a message into the tapestry? Well, it did so much good for who I was trying to help . . . I want to do it again."

"She's right," Ryan piped up. "This is what she wants to do with gift before- well, you know."

We all knew what "Well, you know" really meant. We all dreaded it. We all understood.

Chapter 27

The next morning at school as I walked down the hallway to get to first period, I was halted by the sound of feet rapidly hitting the tile floor and someone calling my name.

"Lucy! Lucy, wait up!"

I turned to see Lacy running towards me, tears running down her face again. But instead of frowning, her mouth was beaming.

"What is it?" I asked, barely managing to conceal what I was thinking, hoping, praying for.

"You won't believe it, Lucy. You won't believe it because I didn't either. But then, I looked outside and there it was!"

"There what was?" I urged. The suspense was killing me, though I already knew the answer.

"Up in the sky . . . *the stars spelled out a message*! My mother saw it and almost fainted, and then my father saw it too! And I thought they were both going crazy . . . but then, I looked and I saw it! They literally said, 'You are Mr. and Mrs. Gardener. Stay that way for Lacy'!"

I finally allowed myself a grin. "That's . . . incredible, Lacy."

She nodded vigorously. "I know! It's a miracle! They think it's a sign! They've both decided they're going to try and work things out- getting divorced almost doesn't seem like an option anymore!"

We probably would've gone on talking for hours... but the bell declared we had a minute to get to class. Lacy left me with a wave and another one of her sweet, genuine smiles before hurrying to art class

Chapter 28

Just like most people with stage four cancer, the goal wasn't to save my life- it was too late for that. The thing everyone- doctors, my friends, Grandfather, myself- were all shooting for was remission, a temporary period of being cancer free. I had been undergoing chemotherapy, but it wasn't really helping much with my symptoms. We had to take it a step further- I was going to have palliative surgery in two weeks.

The entire concept petrified me. Having complete strangers cut into you with knives while you're asleep is not exactly a reassuring notion, at least in my opinion. But the operation would help relieve my pain. It would make what time I had left better and easier to enjoy. The desire to reach that goal helped in part to silence my fear.

Two days before the operation. I was strolling through the park, trying desperately to clear my head. The apprehension was getting to me, and I needed some time to be alone. I didn't even feel like seeing the other Starweavers.

I looked around, trying to let the beauty of the place drown out my apprehension. It was that time of year when the trees were beginning to paint themselves in dazzling shades of crimson and carrot, but still clung resolutely to bits of olive green here and there, and when the air was just starting to carry a chilly note.

Autumn. It was the season I had first received that embroidery box, first reached for the same library book as Jonah, had become a Starweaver . . . had it really been only a year? So much had changed in so little time . . .

I sat down on a bench underneath a tree, trying to take it all in. The memories washed over me like water, immersing me in the warm embrace of happier times.

But I was quite rudely awakened from them by the sound of someone sitting down beside me. I turned to see an ancient looking woman, older than my grandfather, calmly seated next to me. She stared off into the distance, her large, round eyes focusing on seemingly nothing and her thin, stick like fingers clutching a brown paper bag. I decided to ignore her- perhaps she would leave soon.

But of course, *that* wasn't going to happen. She opened the paper bag, seeming completely unaware of my presence, and took out . . . a handful of bread crumbs. She scattered them all over the ground before us, and in minutes, sparrows were feasting at our feet.

"You want feed?" The woman asked in broken English, turning suddenly to me. Her accent was like Grandfather's, only much thicker.

"Sure," I responded in Russian as I took a handful of crumbs and threw them to the birds. Something about it put me at ease, made me feel innocent and peaceful.

The old woman, who still sat next to me, quietly stared at me with a nostalgic, loving warmth in her eyes. When I looked back, I saw that a kind smile had spread itself out over the withered features.

"You remind me of my daughter, Tania," she told me in Russian. "She was your age long ago. She would feed the birds with me just like this when we lived in Moscow"

"Oh . . ." I answered, sounding unsure even to myself. "What happened to her?"

The woman's smile faded and her eyes became cloudy and aloof, like she was remembering something unpleasant. "There was . . . an argument. A silly dispute between us. Silly, and yet very serious. She became so angry she ran here, to America, without my knowledge. I have been trying to find her for years now, but never had any luck. No doubt it is because she does not want to be found. She likely resents me."

I shook my head. "No. She can't resent you. You're her mother. Just because she doesn't want to admit it doesn't mean she doesn't care about you."

She nodded. "Perhaps. But what would you do if your mother tried to keep you working in the same poor, family business for the rest of your life? If she denied you the freedom you had more than earned for yourself?"

I shrugged. "I don't know. I don't have one anymore." My voice had unconsciously dropped to almost a whisper.

The old woman gazed at me, face filled with compassion. Softly, she laid a hand on my arm.

"A motherless daughter and daughterless mother," she mused poetically with a melancholy, nostalgic chuckle as we watched the sparrows gobble up their meal together.

Chapter 29

Even though it was only the third time I had put messages into the tapestry, my friends had grown completely used to it. They did not seem confused as they watched me finish off the blocky Russian letters like they had the first few times. But they still had questions.

"Why does it work?" Jonah asked me a little later. We were down in the library after a night's work, drinking tea and chatting as rain slashed against the glass window panes. "Sewing words into the tapestries? Why do people listen to whatever you put in there?"

I shrugged. "Different reasons. Most people think it's a sign from God. I think Cornelius was right- people look to the stars for hope, so when they see something spelled out especially for them . . . it has an impact. And not just on them- think of all the other people indirectly involved. For example, the first message. That didn't just change Jenny and Ian. Think about the whole Vilkins family, or of the friends and classmates whose lives were altered so drastically just because he came home. It has a ripple effect to it- the people I write the messages to are just the beginning links of an incredibly long chain, details within the big picture."

"Makes sense," Jonah murmured thoughtfully, almond-shaped eyes now focused on the steam rising from his drink.

"So, your surgery . . . what exactly is it gonna do?" Ryan asked me as he lifted the porcelain cup to his lips.

"It's going to relieve my symptoms, at least a little," I responded, pouring some milk from a little pitcher into my tea. "Less pain. A more or less stable body weight. That sort of thing."

"Is there any hope it might save your life?" Jonah asked.

". . . No. It's too late for that."

Chapter 30

The day of the surgery finally came. As I pulled on a cardigan, preparing to leave for the hospital, my phone lit up with a text. To my surprise, it was Jonah's face that illuminated the screen, not Ryan's.

"Good luck. From both of us."

I allowed myself to smile. It was nice to know they cared, even when I wasn't with them.

The drive to the hospital was a silent one on both my grandfather's and my own part. There was nothing to say, not really. Ordinarily, in a situation like this, Grandfather would be offering me wisdom and support. But he was different now; the diagnosis had changed him.

I couldn't help but think about what Mom would have done if she had been alive to see this. Would she have held my hand like she had when I was small, letting her touch quell my fears? Would she have made some sort of empowering, inspirational speech to tell me to keep pushing onward? Or would she have been like how her father was now- sad and solemn and confused?

In the waiting room, decorated with the pastel images of teddy bears, sailboats, ragdolls, and other vintage-looking toys, we sat together, next to a young woman, who looked to be no older than twenty or so, and her child, probably two or three. I had just unfolded a magazine I had scavenged from the rack, when the little boy ambled up to stare at me. I noticed for the first time that his lips were slightly misshapen, like they were made of clay and someone had let a baby try sculpting them.

"Casey, come here!" his mother commanded. She looked up at me. "Sorry," she mumbled as she took her son's hand.

"No, it's okay. Really," I answered laughingly. "Your son is so cute."

"Thank you," the young woman answered, smiling just a bit. "He's pretty high maintenance. This is his second operation."

"Oh? I'm just going in for my first."

"What for?"

"Palliative surgery to help me deal with my pancreatic cancer."

The woman looked horrified, embarrassed and guilty she had asked at all.

"No, no, it's fine," I hastily reassured her. "We're all in the same boat here. I'm sure your family-"

"What family?" she said, cutting me off mid-sentence. "My boyfriend left us as soon as he found out about the cleft lip. My parents hate me for getting pregnant at all . . . he's the only one I have left." She looked sadly at Casey as he toddled around the waiting room, his cookie-round face aglow as he soaked everything in with the pure, blissfully ignorant curiosity of childhood.

I gently placed a hand on his mother's thigh. "Don't worry," I whispered. "It'll be okay. Trust me."

Before she could reply, a nurse stepped into the room. "Lucy Penstark."

I inhaled deeply, trying to steady my nerves as I stood up. It was time.

"Good luck," the woman next to me said.

"Thank you," I answered before following the nurse out of the cheerily painted room and into a sharply contrasting pristine white corridor.

Chapter 31

"Well, are you gonna help us eat this or not, birthday girl?" Ryan asked playfully from the hospital room's doorway, carrying a little cardboard box in his hands. Just behind him, Jonah, eyes glowing like a cat's, clutched a plastic bag.

"Of course." I could feel the sappy grin forming on my face as each boy took a seat next to me.

Ryan opened up the box and produced a very small cake, decorated with snowy, lace-like frosting and ruby red strawberries as bright and sweet as candy. Mint green icing spelled out the simple yet kind-hearted words "Happy birthday and get well soon."

"That's not a suggestion. It's an order." Jonah said as he cut the treat into thirds and carefully levered the slices onto paper plates.

"I don't know if I'll be able to follow that one." I responded, taking a plastic fork from the bag.

"You'd better," Ryan said jokingly as he took a mammoth bite of cake. "We'd be lost without you."

'Well, get ready to be lost,' I thought miserably.

"How are you feeling?" Ryan probed. "The surgery was a few days ago, right?"

I nodded. "Kind of sore . . . and very tired. But, I'm okay otherwise. Apparently, went pretty well. They'll just keep me here for a week."

"Good," Jonah said sternly, jaw firmly set with determination. "You can start coming back to Night Hall again after that, but for now, we'll use the embroidery boxes again."

The morning sky was still a light shade of dappled gray- far too early to be eating cake, even if I was turning seventeen. My pain had only subsided a little bit, my abdomen was stiff with gauze, and we scattered crumbs all over the clean, white sheets, but I didn't care. It felt so good to simply relax on my birthday, celebrating quietly with the people I loved after all that had happened. I now savored the moment every bit as much as the pleasant combination of vanilla and strawberry in my mouth.

I gazed at the large apple tree outside my window as I finished sewing in the message to the woman I had met the day before. It looked tall and majestic in the sunlight, so strong and steadfast, yet simultaneously beautiful and picturesque, like an illustration in a book. I had wished when I first laid eyes on it that I too could possess that same quiet, noble strength- and that others, like little Casey and his mother, could as well.

In a way, I had begun to grow in that area. When I first saw Ian come back to Jenny, witnessed with my own eyes the joy I had elicited, I began to understand that each detail, both the positive and the negative, had combined to produce a stronger, better person in the end. Maybe being me- cancer patient, Starweaver, and all- wasn't really so bad.

Chapter 32

The soft, hurried sound of my pen flying over paper in a kind of wild, rushed dance was all there was to be heard in the little hospital room as I poured my heart onto the pages of the purple and black notebook, allowing the words to reflect my feelings as clearly and uncompromisingly as a mirror. There was something eerily comforting in the liberation writing that entry made me feel- a deeply emotional, heartfelt letter full of pain and regret, addressed to someone who would never read it should not have given me so much peace. But it did.

Dear Mom,

All my life you told me I was special. You loved me because I was one of a kind. Because I stood out from the crowd. For as long as I can remember, you tried to convince me that being myself- someone different- wasn't a shameful curse, but a welcome gift. And I never listened. You never stopped telling me that message over and over again with your kind, inspirational voice, but it fell on stubborn, deaf ears every single time. And then, one rainy April night, the voice was unexpectedly silenced.

In the past year, though, I've been hearing that same message in the same voice again. The one that preached that I was talented, and unique, and important in its constant, tranquil way. And I am an idiot, because only now, that I am about to die, do I finally realize what was in front of me this whole time; that that voice, explaining that message, was correct. That YOU were correct.

I'm sorry. I'm so, so sorry that I didn't listen. I'm sorry that I came to my senses too late. I'm sorry that it took all of this to finally learn my lesson. I deeply, sincerely apologize for everything. And I know it's a bit too late, but it feels good to say it all the same. Your eternally grateful daughter, Lucy.

Tears spouted from my eyes. It wasn't the first time I had written to Mom like that and cried over it- journaling had been something Grandfather had suggested to help cope with her death. But it was the first time that the tears which stained the page and smeared the words into messy blobs had been filled with more than just plain sorrow- this time, they had been born of a strange, spookily final sense of serenity. I felt I had at last made the proper amends- that I'd finally sealed off my deepest, darkest emotions surrounding one of the defining experiences of my life.

Chapter 33

"Come on, Lucy. Let's go," Ryan urged as he pulled me by the arm outside Night Hall and through the dewy blades of grass at our feet.

"What's going on? What are we doing?" I asked as he dragged me along.

"Sailing one last time," Jonah, a little way in front of us, answered.

"That's right!" Ryan exclaimed. "We wanted to take you one last time. While we still could . . ." His voice trailed off, but I understood exactly what he meant.

We made our way down to cave and soon found ourselves aboard the beloved ship once again.

"Lucy, would you like to do the honors?" Ryan asked, holding out the wind string to me. I nodded, taking the silver cord eagerly.

"Brace yourselves," I cautioned before slowly, carefully, untying a knot.

We were all far more used to the jolt of the ship as it began moving than we had been the first time we sailed, on my sixteenth birthday. But even so, we were very nearly thrown off of our feet. I clung to the mast and Jonah to me and Ryan to the wheel as we felt it accelerate and rise up, climbing higher and higher into the night air. I could have reached out and touched one of the stars in the Mosaic.

We gracefully glided through the sky, feeling wondrously free and content as we soared through the night. We passed over charming, quaint little homes, lush forests with golden leaves adorning the trees, lively flower fields, a large, tranquil lagoon, shimmering like a gem in the moonlight. Great white swans floated across the water with their slender arched necks and majestic wings. I felt so powerful, and yet so very peaceful as we sailed over the landscape; I even forgot about my cancer. I glanced to either side of me- to Ryan, so energetic and bright, always ready to comfort me in times of trouble. And to Jonah, always calm, cool, and collected, offering me wisdom and insight whenever I needed it. In that moment, I was so grateful for their presence, so glad I was experiencing this with them . . . I didn't want it to ever end.

Chapter 34

"Ah! These cookies you made are excellent, malen'kiy," Grandfather announced as he practically inhaled one of the sweets I had baked several hours earlier, this one shaped like a wreath. Christmas Eve had snuck up on us yet again, and we had nearly forgotten it with all that had been happening. My condition had started worsening again, with pain now becoming far sharper and lasting longer, and I even came close to fainting several times. In all of that, we had nearly forgotten Christmas Eve. Nearly.

"Thanks," I responded, biting into a cookie resembling a stocking. It was something of a messy bite, one that got bits of sugar on my cherry red sweater, but I didn't care; the other Starweavers had invited me to a second Christmas Eve party at Night Hall, and this time, I had prepared a present and a card for each.

I could still recall their exact expressions upon hearing I would attend. Cornelius had smiled gruffly and offered a small chuckle, clearly pleased, happy, even, and yet reluctant to come out and say it. Ryan had instantly reminded me of a jack-o-lantern; an eager, too-big-for-his-face, grin, and oddly enough, an identical warm glow that seemed to come from his innermost being. And Jonah- it wasn't often he showed such emotion outwardly, but when he did, it was something worth waiting for, a precious little spark of joy just reminding me that he was, indeed, my friend and cared about me deeply. I smiled to myself just at the thought of how they would react to my gifts.

"Would you mind getting the milk for me?" Grandfather asked, pulling me from my imaginings.

"Sure," I answered, rising from my place at the table and making my way to the refrigerator. I looked out the kitchen window; countless snowflakes were falling smoothly onto the soft white blanket outside, adding bit by bit to its mass.

I began to dream of what the weather at Star Rock would be like. It might provide a significant, yet much appreciated contrast to where I was, like it had a year ago. I recalled that day now; the sun had sent its rays down to us as though they were Christmas presents, the ocean waves had grabbed at the sandy shore to just before dissolving into seafoam, and the brilliantly colored flowers that flecked the grassy field had appeared to be in the full splendor of spring.

I reached for the milk carton, now only half aware I was holding it. I was completely immersed in my reverie, so much so my hand barely realized the cold of the refrigerator.

But I did suddenly become frighteningly aware of a startling, dizzy feeling, very rapidly beginning to overtake me. I had felt it before, but never quite so strongly as I did now, never enough to truly scare me. It became harder to put one foot in front of the other as my vision blurred, sending me only a fuzzy image of the black and white checkered floor. I felt myself panicking as I fought for control over myself, trying to force myself to stay awake, screaming at myself that I was fine.

'Come on, come on!' my thoughts shouted at me, 'Stay awake! Not now! You can't let your friends down!'

But it was all in vain. I felt the milk carton slip from my fingers, heard its contents splash onto the floor by my feet, wetting my stockings through. I felt myself collapse, falling hard onto the tile, hitting my cheek. It hurt. The cold milk ran into my hair, but I didn't care. I couldn't care. I faintly heard Grandfather calling to me in a worried voice, asking if I was all right, but no sound came to my throat. I didn't have the strength to respond. Instead, I used what little energy I had left to think.

'Don't you dare do this. Don't you dare pass out. Not on yourself. Not on your grandfather. Not on your friends. You still have a party to go to, remember? You still have gifts to give, food to eat, people to laugh alongside . . . just hang on. Just a little bit longer. You

have to see them. Just one last time. Even for just a second each. Just

one last time . . . stay awake . . . stay awake . . . stay awake . . .'

Chapter 35

Smooth, cool sheets trapped my body in their grip. I was now stretched out on a bed, but not my own. I recognized where I was without even opening my eyes; a hospital room. Lids still shut, I absorbed the too-sanitary scent, feeling of an IV tube sticking out of my arm, rhythmic beeping of a machine close by . . . and the sound of someone speaking in a shaky, agonized voice- Grandfather.

"I'm so sorry . . . I completely let you down. You are an amazing young lady; so bright and full of life, and yet soft, quiet and gentle . . . just like your mother." He must have thought I was still asleep, poor man!

The discovery of my cancer had come between us. There was less time to do things we usually did together, and constant stress on both of our parts had not exactly helped the situation. It had been just as hard for him as for me.

"You can't mean that," I said weakly, opening my eyes with some effort. He gazed up at me in surprise, tears glistening as they sat in his ocean colored eyes.

"Oh, but I do," he said grimly. "You deserved so much... better than what I gave you. I should have been there for you, shown you all the support and love and protection you needed. But I didn't. I was too blind . . . blinded by grief and confusion and stress . . . and only now am I able to finally admit it. I'm sorry."

I shook my head. "It wasn't your fault. You *were* blind. And now, you're seeing."

Neither of us said anything for a moment before I continued.

"Those words you used to describe me earlier... do you think any of them could possibly have come to *anyone's* minds when thinking of me if you hadn't taken me in after Mom died? The words that they'd probably use would have been 'Depressed. Reclusive. Unlikeable.' If you were able to raise me into someone who brings *those* words to mind, I'd say you did a pretty good job."

The old man stood up on his wobbly legs to hug me, hobbling unsteadily to my bedside and wrapping his skinny arms around my frail frame. I felt his tears run into my hair and allowed my own to wet his shirt. It reminded me of when I was younger and he first moved into the apartment to take care of me. I would have nightmares about my mother's accident, horrific, terrifying dreams that ended with me waking up screaming and drenched in sweat. But every single time, Grandfather had comforted me, did his best to calm my fears.

He had been too grief stricken to calm me during most of *this* nightmare until just this minute. And now that he had, at this time right before the end of my life, it was so very valuable to me- like all that had been cold and dead between us was suddenly all right again.

Chapter 36

Maybe it was selfish. Maybe I could've let them figure it out on their own. Maybe I could have chosen not to take up their time, to not disrupt their festivities. But I didn't want to do that. I wanted, needed, to see my friends just one last time.

I sent them each a simple, identical text; 'In hospital. Please come before too late.'

I leaned back against the pillow, just hoping, praying, that they'd receive it. Just this last time. This one final time.

Four minutes dragged by. I could feel my breath slow, each one taking considerably more effort as my heart rate decreased, causing the machine's beeps to come at longer intervals. The pain in my abdomen, which had been present all this time, had been somewhat dulled by painkillers, dulled, but not silenced.

I felt that I was losing control, fighting a losing battle for consciousness as I had just before passing out in the kitchen. My vision blurred, not only from delirium, but from the tears that had gathered in my eyes as well upon coming across the tragic, unavoidable revelation; not that I was dying. I could handle that. Not that I was dying, but that I would never be able to say goodbye to Jonah and Ryan.

The images of my room and Grandfather were now mere colored blurs. His soothing, deep voice was now scarcely more than a low humming in my ears. It was all finally coming to a close.

Memories now flooded into my head, like a dam holding back a raging river had at last burst. I thought of my mother, my grandfather, Jenny, Lacy, Casey and his mother, the Russian woman in the park, Cornelius . . . and of Ryan and Jonah. Their faces all filled what little time I had left before I quietly, slowly, closed my eyes, and at long last relinquished control, letting the deep, dark embrace of sleep wash over me with its warm, deafening silence.

Chapter 37

The two figures of the boys, wrapped heavily in winter coats, stood rooted in the middle of the snowy graveyard like trees, looking down at their friend's tombstone. Each held his own card and present from her.

Jonah's long, knobby fingers held a small, yet beautiful, snow globe. Inside, was a tiny piano amidst the snowflakes, jet black and solitary. The base of the snow globe had been carved with intricate, ornate designs, reminiscent of musical sheet music with notes dancing up and down the staff.

With it came a card, reading in Lucy's cursive handwriting, 'Merry Christmas, Jonah! Thanks for always keeping me sane and being there for me when I needed you- Lucy!'

It had taken all of Jonah's self-control to keep from bursting into tears upon finding it, but even so, he had not been able to stop one from rolling down his cheek.

It had surprised him, that single, little tear. His entire life, he had been able to divorce himself from emotions, keep everything bottled up deep inside. And yet, something about Lucy had changed that. She had been someone who made him *feel*. Joy, excitement, sympathy, protectiveness, concern, inspiration, love . . . and now immense, gripping pain as he stood there staring down at her shining ebony tombstone, emblazoned with golden letters spelling out a brief description of one more remarkable person the world now lacked.

Ryan was right next to him, clutching his own present- a little Christmas tree ornament shaped like a soccer ball, with fire engine red- his favorite color- hexagons in place of the usual black ones.

The card Lucy had written for him had said, 'Thank you for making me smile when nothing else could. Merry Christmas- Lucy!'

He now recalled his friend as she had been that memorable afternoon, when she had spoken so sternly to him as he sat on the stone steps with a twisted ankle, abundant vegetation, the ancient manor, and the tangy fragrance of the ocean all remarkably vivid and fresh in his mind. And then, of course, there had been the girl, outlined against a tangerine sky, chestnut hair framing her passionate face. That orange day had found him totally lost and confused and morose, too proud to ask for help, and yet too desperate to refuse it, like a child left without his parents in a busy mall. In that moment, Lucy, his quiet, insecure companion, had been a fiery star of hope brightly burning during one of one of his darkest hours, a strong and steady lighthouse in the middle of a stormy sea. She never in a million years would have seen herself as strong- but he had that afternoon.

"Why?"

Jonah's harsh, angry voice broke into Ryan's thoughts.

"Why did she have to die?" He spat the words out with bitter rage. "She was just seventeen . . . and so good. So gentle, and intelligent, and funny, and kind. And now, she's gone. Just like that. Why?"

Ryan shrugged. "I don't know."

"And no one ever will."

The boys whirled around to face Cornelius, who had come up from behind them.

"No one will ever know for certain," the Teacher continued, "But I do have my opinion. If Lucy had not been in the condition she was in, think of all the lives that could have been so much worse. Jenny Vilkins, Lacy Gardener, and so many others . . . they would never have been touched by the miracles Lucy sewed into the sky."

He placed one hand on either boy's shoulder. "Lucy Anastasia Penstark was not a great person because nothing bad ever happened to her, or because she never faced any challenges, but because she took all of those horrible things in her life and transformed them into reasons and opportunities to use her gift for wonderful, beautiful things, much greater than she herself could ever be. The world would be a much better place if there were more people who had the courage and the wisdom to follow her example."

With one final parting glance at the tombstone, he led his two pupils away. "Come. Without her, there will be much more work to be done at Night Hall. Let's get started."

Epilogue

Every Christmas Eve night, year after year, that mirthless wintry graveyard, cold and still with the heavy coat of darkness thrown over its shoulders, is illuminated by the soft, silvery starlight of a very special constellation. The stars burn with an intense, yet lovely fire. The radiant dots of light are arranged intricately in complex, beautiful patterns. It is unique. Distinct. One-of-a-kind.

No one can agree on what it means, or how it came to be, or why it even exists at all. But the one thing no one dares dispute is that the stars form the shape of a slim, wavy-haired girl, sitting at a loom as she weaves a tapestry, with a bright smile resting peacefully on her face in some obscure, anonymous Christmas gift to someone long since gone from this world, but never to be forgotten up in the night sky.